Reading Essentials® in Science

THE WEATHER REPORT

Erosion

VIRGINIA CASTLEMAN

PERFECTION LEARNING®

Editorial Director: Susan C. Thies
Editor: Judith A. Bates
Design Director: Randy Messer
Book Design: Michelle Glass, Brianne Osborn
Cover Design: Mike Aspengren

A special thanks to the following for her scientific
review of the book:

Judy Beck, Ph.D.
Associate professor, science education
University of South Carolina-Spartanburg

IMAGE CREDITS:

Associated Press: p. 33 (left); ©Peter Barrett/CORBIS: p. 5;
©Joe McDonald/CORBIS: p. 9; ©CORBIS: p. 11 (top left);
©Philip Gould/CORBIS: p. 11 (bottom left); ©Reuters NewMedia
Inc./CORBIS: p. 11 (right); ©CORBIS: p. 21; ©Bettmann/CORBIS:
pp. 24–25; ©Niall Benvie/CORBIS: pp. 27 (top); ©Bettmann/CORBIS:
pp. 35 (bottom)

Royalty-Free/Corbis: pp. 4 (left), 31, 34; PhotoDisc: pp. 29, 32, 35 (top), 37;
Photos.com: Front and back cover, pp. 2–3, 4 (right), 6, 7, 8, 10 (bottom),
12, 14, 16, 17, 19, 23, 26, 27 (bottom), 28, 30, 33 (right), 36, 38–39, 40;
MapArt™: pp. 18, 22; Perfection Learning Corporation: 10, 13, 20

For information, contact
Perfection Learning® Corporation
1000 North Second Avenue, P.O. Box 500
Logan, Iowa 51546-0500.
Phone: 1-800-831-4190
Fax: 1-800-543-2745
perfectionlearning.com
5 6 7 8 9 10 LT 11 10 09 08 07 06
ISBN 0-7891-6116-8
Reinforced Library Binding ISBN 0-7569-4441-4

Contents

Grand Canyon

Millions of years of eros
formed Death Valley's ha
desert environm

Introduction

Have you ever watered a garden and held the hose in one spot for too long? What happened? Did some of the dirt around the plants float away with the water? What you saw is erosion.

Have you ever visited or seen pictures of the Grand Canyon? Did you wonder how it formed? The Grand Canyon is a product of erosion.

Have you ever been in a sandstorm at the beach or seen pictures of sand dunes in the desert? These are examples of erosion too.

Erosion is the removal of rock and soil **particles** by nature. The main natural movers are water, ice, and wind. These are aided by temperature and gravity. So you see, weather plays a major part in erosion.

Earth is changing every day as a result of erosion. In most cases, erosion happens so slowly that you don't even notice. But at times, such as during a heavy downpour, erosion can take place immediately.

Erosion is a natural process. But over the years, human activity has increased the amount and the speed of erosion. **Environmental** steps are being taken to correct problems relating to erosion. Sometimes the answers are simple. At other times, they're not. But they all lead to one solution—preserving Earth.

1

What's Weather Got to Do with It?

Ah, ah, ah! Don't blame weathercasters if the weather is rotten. They only track and report the weather. They don't make it. Snow days can be fun if you get to miss school. And hot days are great for going swimming. But weather affects more than just activities.

Weather has a lot to do with erosion. Rain, ice, and wind are weather conditions that lead to and cause erosion.

But before erosion can occur, rocks need to be broken down into particles. **Geologists** refer to this process as **weathering**. Weathering can occur by itself. Erosion can only happen after weathering has taken place.

Weathering

Water soaks them. Extreme temperatures crack them. Ice freezes in their cracks. Wind wears them away. **Acid** rain eats them up. Can you guess what "they" are? If you guessed rocks, you're absolutely right!

There are three types of rock—sedimentary, igneous, and metamorphic. Weather breaks down sedimentary rock more easily than it does the other two types of rock.

Weathering vs. Erosion

Weathering is the natural breakdown of rocks into particles, usually by rain, ice, and wind. The particles become soil and don't move. Erosion is the gradual wearing away of rock or soil and the moving of that material to another place.

Just remember! If a rock is chipped away and the particles stay put, the process is weathering. If particles start moving, it's erosion.

Know Your Rocks

Sedimentary rocks are formed by layers of **sediments**. These sediments pile on top of one another for thousands of years. The weight, or pressure, of the top layers causes the bottom layers to bond, or stick together, to form solid rock. Examples of sedimentary rocks are sandstone, limestone, and coal.

Igneous rocks are formed from magma, a hot liquid rock found between Earth's crust and core. Magma works its way up into the crust where it cools and hardens. If the magma breaks through the surface, it's called *lava*. Granite, basalt, obsidian, and pumice are examples of igneous rocks.

Metamorphic rocks are sedimentary or igneous rocks that have been changed into different rocks by extreme heat and pressure. For example, limestone turns to marble, and shale turns into slate. These rocks usually form when mountains are created.

Sandstone

Granite

Marble

Weathering occurs on or near Earth's surface. Rocks are beaten by rain, torn apart by ice, and tortured by wind. Small particles are worn off the rocks, becoming soil.

Geologists study two types of weathering—mechanical and chemical.

Rock

When geologists refer to rock, they aren't always talking about rocks like those found on the playground or in a driveway. They are usually talking about all rock from pebbles to mountains.

Mechanical Weathering

Mechanical weathering breaks apart rock without changing the chemical makeup of its **minerals**. One of the main causes of mechanical weathering is ice. Water soaks into the cracks of rocks. As temperatures fall below 32°F, the water freezes and **expands**. It pushes out hard enough to cause the crack to grow. As temperatures warm, the ice melts and the crack **contracts**. In only a few short years, a rock can be reduced to tiny particles by the constant expanding and contracting. This process is called *frost wedging*.

Fill a small plastic container, such as a yogurt container, to the top with water. Replace the lid, and put the container in a freezer for 24 hours. Check the container. What happened? Did the ice force the lid off the container? Or did the container split? The ice expanded, so it needed more space. The pressure of the expanding ice forced the lid off the container, or in some cases, actually split the container. This is what happens when ice freezes inside a rock.

Tree and plant roots weather rocks in the same manner as ice does. The roots work their way into cracks. As they grow, they split the rocks into small pieces. Then insects, worms, reptiles, and mammals walk and dig on Earth's surface where these broken rocks lie. The particles are crushed and loosened even more, making it easy for them to be blown or washed away.

Chemical Weathering

Chemical weathering involves a chemical change in at least some of the minerals within a rock. Substances such as water and acids get into rocks and react with the minerals that make up the rock.

One of the main causes of chemical weathering is water. Rain, streams, rivers, and seawater dissolve some minerals from rocks, making the rocks weaker. One such mineral is iron. Oxygen combines with iron and changes it to iron oxide, or rust. Water combines with minerals to form new compounds by a process called *hydration*. Feldspar is changed into clay by hydration.

Weathering continues every minute of every day. But what happens when weathered material is rained on, frozen, or blown around? After enough time, the minerals change enough that the rock finally crumbles.

Rocks are weathered by the Lamar River in Yellowstone National Park.

Try This!

Collect small, broken pieces of soft rocks, such as sandstone, shale, or limestone. Place some of the rocks in a large plastic container. A plastic juice bottle works best. Set the remainder of the rocks aside.

Fill the bottle about halfway with clear water. Close the lid of the bottle and shake it for 10 to 15 minutes. You might want to do this with a partner or small group. It's fun to play some of your favorite rap or rock music while you do this.

Remove the rocks and note any changes in their appearance compared with the rocks that were set aside.

Examine the water. Is it still clear? Strain the water through a paper coffee filter. Do you see any sediments?

This is how rocks in streams are weathered by water and their movement. You might want to try this experiment with other rocks and compare the results.

Erosion occurs when these particles are carried away to another place.

The wind can carry topsoil for miles as shown in this 1930s photo of a dust storm.

A Costa Rican man cleans a street in his village after a 2002 mudslide.

Heavy waves wash around the bases of telephone poles near Galveston, Texas. The beach has eroded, and the poles now stand in water. Even the nearby road is growing smaller.

Erosion

Erosion is the natural process in which weathered rock and soil on Earth's surface is picked up in one location and moved to another. This has been happening since Earth was formed more than 4 billion years ago.

After rocks have weathered, raindrops splash on the land and carry soil downhill. Glaciers cause erosion by moving soil that is **embedded** in them. Winds also cause erosion by lifting the particles from Earth's surface and carrying them great distances.

Erosion is usually a slow process, taking thousands to millions of years. Erosion forms and changes land. It wears down mountains and fills in valleys. Erosion makes rivers appear and disappear.

But there are times when erosion happens quickly. Too much rain on an already wet hillside can result in a mudslide. Or a fierce wind in a desert can form sand dunes that change the entire surface of the sand.

Weather—rain or snow, ice, and wind—provides the "vehicles" to move soil particles causing erosion.

11

Water Erosion

Water Cycle

In order to understand water erosion, you need to understand the water cycle.

Water is plentiful on Earth. In fact, more than 71 percent of the planet is covered by water. But where does this water come from?

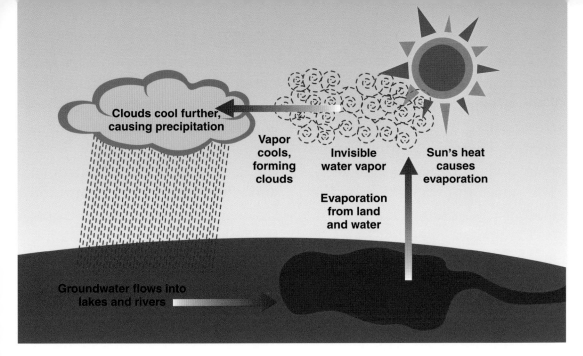

Clouds cool further, causing precipitation

Vapor cools, forming clouds

Invisible water vapor

Sun's heat causes evaporation

Evaporation from land and water

Groundwater flows into lakes and rivers

Rain and snow are part of the water cycle. The Sun heats Earth. Water in puddles, lakes, rivers, on plants, and even in the air begins to **evaporate**. These **vapors** rise, cool, and **condense**. Wind tosses the small particles of water around, and they begin to cling to specks of dust and form droplets. The droplets then join together, forming clouds. When the clouds contain more drops than they can hold, the drops fall to the ground as precipitation. The water fills the puddles, lakes, and rivers. This is a process that happens over and over and over and . . . Well, you get the idea.

Rivers and Streams

Water erosion occurs when an area receives more water, in the form of rain, melting snow, or ice, than it can **absorb**. The **excess** water flows over the ground and quickly turns brown as it takes rocks and other loose weathered material with it. The farther it moves, the more rocks and particles it picks up. The rocks and particles are carried to a lower spot where they are **deposited**.

How Much?

Every year, rivers deposit about 3.5 million tons of soil, rocks, and other eroded materials into the oceans.

Rainwater and snowmelt drain from the land into streams. The streams flow downhill to rivers that flow downhill to oceans. The moving water wears away soil and rock as it travels. The faster the water moves, the more it erodes the land around it.

Erosion on gentle slopes is much less than the erosion on steeper hills and mountains. On small slopes, water moves more slowly. Only a thin layer of **topsoil** is removed. This erosion is balanced by weathering, which creates new soil.

Erosion on steeper hills and mountains is more severe. As the water rushes downhill, **gullies** and **rivulets** form. Since water seems to follow the same path, the gullies and rivulets deepen and widen as water cuts into the surface. One of the finest examples of this type of erosion is the Grand Canyon.

More than 2 million years ago, the Colorado River flowed on the surface of the ground. It was just like a stream of water running down your driveway. But over time, the river has eroded the ground. Now it lies almost a mile below the surface in a huge canyon.

The Grand Canyon became a National Park in 1919. It covers 1,218,375 acres of land in northwestern Arizona. The Grand Canyon hosts more than five million visitors per year.

The Grand Canyon

When the Grand Canyon was formed, the Colorado River was mainly responsible for its depth. Wind and rain pounding on the sides of the canyon are two of the factors responsible for its width.

The Grand Canyon is one of the most studied geologic places in the world. The rock walls of the canyon show how Earth has formed. At the bottom is **schist** that is more than 2 billion years old. At the top is 250-million-year-old limestone. These rocks help scientists determine Earth's age and learn more about how it formed. Fossils tell scientists when some of the first life appeared.

The Grand Canyon is considered one of the best examples of water erosion in the world. This natural wonder is almost 6000 feet deep at its deepest point and 15 miles wide at its widest point.

Acid Rain

Let's go back to the water cycle. Remember how rain falls from clouds when the clouds are too full? As rain falls, the drops pick up gases in the air, creating a chemical reaction and forming acid. Carbon dioxide is in the air because it's a product of breathing. So rain contains some acid, but that's okay. The mild acid acts as chemical weathering of rocks, providing **nutrients** to the soil.

But in the last 100 years, the air has become more **polluted** with sulfur dioxide and nitrogen dioxide. Sulfur dioxide can come from natural sources such as volcanoes. But today, most of this gas is released into the air by factories that burn coal and oil. Nitrogen dioxide comes from car exhaust and power stations. Rain that absorbs these gases contains higher levels of acid. Rains with high amounts of acid break down minerals too quickly. The minerals that provide nutrients disappear. The result—plants can't grow and hold the soil in place. Land becomes barren, and erosion begins.

Oceans

All along coastlines, waves and tides continually change the shape of the land. They wear away rocky shores much like an eraser wears away a pencil line. Sandbars, beaches, and rocky cliffs are left behind. This erosion takes millions of years. But during hurricanes and other severe storms, waves beat the shoreline harder, so erosion happens more quickly.

Flooding

Some years, heavy winter snowfalls are followed by spring downpours. This may be more than the ground can absorb. What happens to all the runoff? It goes into streams and rivers that are already too full. The result is flooding. Floodwaters spread over the nearby lands, picking up soil and rocks. As the waters move away, they carry many more soil particles than are moved during a normal rain.

3

Ice
Erosion

You already read about how ice weathers rocks. But ice also moves soil and rock. It causes erosion and changes in Earth's surface. This ice is usually in the form of **glaciers**.

Today you can find glaciers high in mountains throughout the world. Greenland is almost entirely covered by a glacier, and Antarctica is just one giant glacier.

The yellow areas show
where glaciers are found.

A glacier begins as snowflakes in places where more snow falls than can melt. When the snow piles up, its weight causes the snow at the bottom of the pile to turn to ice. Year after year, the snow falls, and layers build up until a glacier forms. Because of its weight and the slope of the mountain, the glacier is slowly pulled downhill by gravity.

The Iceman

Glaciers move slowly and melt slowly. The discovery of the Iceman demonstrates this.

On September, 19, 1991, two hikers discovered a body in the Alps between Italy and Austria. The well-preserved body was found among the melting water and **debris** of a glacier. Scientists determined the man lived between 3350 and 3100 B.C. To learn more about the man from the glacier, check out **www.mrsedivy.com/iceman2.html**.

Glaciers act like sandpaper. As they move, they scrape and grind the surfaces below them, breaking up rocks and loosening soil. The ice picks up the loosened materials and carries them along the glacier's path, leaving behind bare rock.

Making Land Formations

During the last Ice Age more than 16,000 years ago, glaciers eroded enough of Earth's surface to create hills, valleys, and even the Great Lakes.

As the tip of a glacier reaches warmer, lower land, it begins to melt. Glacial melts can cause rivers and streams to overflow. Weakened snow and ice can result in avalanches. All the soil and rock picked up during the glacier's journey is then deposited somewhere else.

The natural process of erosion happens slowly. It takes hundreds of thousands of years to wear away mountains and carve out valleys and lakes.

19

the sand. Describe what you see. Did any of the sand cling to the ice?

Materials

modeling clay
ice cube
1 spoonful of coarse sand
a paper towel

Procedure

1. Form the modeling clay into a flat circle or square.
2. Press the ice cube lightly on the flat surface of the modeling clay. Move it back and forth several times. Does anything happen to the clay? to the ice?
3. Place a small pile of sand on the surface of the clay.
4. Set the ice cube on the sand. Let it sit for several minutes. Lift the ice cube and look at the surface that had been on

5. Place the ice cube back in the same position, and move it back and forth on the sandy surface of the clay a few times.
6. Remove the ice cube and gently wipe the excess sand from the surface of the clay with a paper towel. Describe the surface of the clay where it was rubbed by the sand and ice. How do you think this would compare with the surface of the land when rock and other materials are dragged over it by a glacier?

20

4

Wind Erosion

It was the time of the Great Depression. The nation was already feeling the pinch of a collapsed economy. Nature decided to add another problem.

In the 1930s, a **drought** hit the Great Plains. Very little rain and extreme heat caused crops and grasslands to dry up. The wind seemed to blow constantly, carrying the rich topsoil hundreds of miles away. By 1934, about 35 million acres of land in the Dust Bowl were stripped. This was one of the worst natural erosion disasters to hit the United States.

Montana
North Dakota
Minnesota
South Dakota
Wyoming
Nebraska
Iowa
Colorado
Kansas
Missouri
Dust Bowl
of the 1930s
New Mexico
Oklahoma
Arkansas
Texas

Other areas damaged
by dust storms

Dust Bowl

The Dust Bowl is the name given to a region of the southwestern United States. During the early 1930s, far less than the normal amount of rain fell in parts of this region. The hardest-hit area included the panhandles of Texas and Oklahoma, southwestern Kansas, and southeastern Colorado. Damage from dust storms spread north into Nebraska, South Dakota, Wyoming, Montana, North Dakota, and New Mexico.

Winds whipped the dust and dirt into the air. These frequent winds blew topsoil clear across the continent to the Atlantic Coast and far out into the Gulf of Mexico. Farmhouses were often hidden behind drifts of dust. People had to wear handkerchiefs or masks to keep the dust out of their mouths, noses, and lungs.

Think of a gentle breeze blowing against your face. It feels soft. But add soil particles and sand, and it becomes abrasive and biting.

Wind is the third major contributor to erosion. Unlike water and ice, wind can only move very small particles. That doesn't mean it's less destructive. There are two types of wind erosion. One is deflation and the other is sandblasting.

Deflation

Deflation is the removal of large quantities of loose materials from an area by the wind. This process usually occurs slowly. But it can happen quickly as it did in the 1930s in the United States. In a sandy desert, the wind can change a familiar landscape into an unknown area during one sandstorm. It can move and rearrange sand dunes in just a short period of time.

Deflation lifts only the tiniest particles of sand and silt and leaves behind larger pebbles and stones. Eventually, a surface layer of closely packed stones called *desert pavement* is formed. This layer protects the surface against further deflation.

Place a shoe box lid in the center of an open sheet of newspaper on a table. Place a cupful of sand in the center of the lid. Blow gently on the sand, increasing the strength of your breath until the sand is being thrown from the lid. Continue blowing for 5 to 10 seconds at this rate.

Examine the material that was blown onto the paper by rubbing your finger over it. Do the same to the material left in the box lid. Are the textures of the sand different or alike? Is one finer than the other?

A man walks past a farmhouse during a dust storm in Oklahoma in 1937.

Sandblasting

Have you ever seen workers blasting paint off a hard surface? The workers use a high-pressure machine to produce a strong windlike force that blasts sand against the surface. That's exactly what nature does with wind and sand. Only nature's way takes much longer.

The walls of the Grand Canyon are blasted every day by winds. These winds loosen soil that is carried away by the Colorado River below or by the winds themselves. This type of erosion has helped make the canyon wider at the top.

Sandblasting happens more in the arid and semi-arid regions of the world.

❋❋❋❋❋❋❋❋❋❋❋❋❋❋❋❋❋❋❋❋❋❋❋❋❋

Today, dust storms are not much of a problem in the United States. But they remain a problem in parts of northern Africa, Asia, and Europe. Conditions such as those that were found in the United States in the 1930s are still present there today.

5
The Effects of Erosion

Erosion can be helpful, beautiful, and harmful. Erosion helps to form soil by breaking up and moving rock. It deposits rich soil on valley floors and at the **mouths** of rivers.

We can see the beauty erosion creates in places such as the Grand Canyon and Bryce Canyon National Park. It's Earth's natural sculptor.

Bryce Canyon National Park

But erosion isn't all help and beauty. In the United States, soil erosion occurs at the rate of 13 tons per 2.5 acres a year. Soil erosion is also a problem in Africa, Asia, and Latin America. Land is left barren and unprotected from rain and wind. Some experts say that in the last 40 years, more than 30 percent of the world's cropland has become unproductive due to erosion.

Soil is a valuable resource on the land, but it's worthless when too much of it ends up in rivers, streams, ponds, lakes, and oceans. The United States contains about 2.3 billion acres of land. Of that amount, only about 460 million acres are considered agricultural land. Wind erosion alone is a major problem on about 75 million acres of agricultural land.

Almost 5 million acres of agricultural land are moderately to severely damaged by all types of erosion each year. In total, about 175 million acres have already been severely damaged.

Soil erosion in a potato field after heavy rains is shown in the photo above. Below is an example of an undamaged field.

Construction site

Soil is a valuable resource. Do you think it's easy to replace? If you said yes, think again. It takes about 500 years to replace 1 inch of topsoil. Farmers need at least 6 inches of topsoil for agricultural production. In the United States, soil is eroding about 17 times faster than it is forming.

Soil erosion has resulted in nutrients being stripped from the soil. To solve this problem, farmers must add nutrients back into the soil. Some of these fertilizers contain harmful chemicals that are eroded just like natural nutrients are. Eroded materials end up in irrigation ditches, ponds, and reservoirs, often polluting our drinking water.

When topsoil and nutrients are lost, farmland becomes useless. When crops won't grow, farmers often just leave plowed fields unplanted. Without plant or tree roots to hold the soil, water and wind can carry away even more topsoil.

In today's world, humans have accelerated the rate of erosion. People clear trees and other **vegetation** from the land to make room for houses, malls, and more farmland. Have you ever been near a construction site on a windy

One-third of Earth's land is covered by forests. Half of these are rain forests where it is believed half of Earth's plants and animals live. At the current rate of deforestation, hundreds of thousands of plants and animals are becoming extinct. If the current rate continues, one quarter of the species may be extinct in 25 years.

day? The wind often whips up so much dirt that you can't even see. From a distance, you can watch the soil roll across the area.

In the United States, 30 percent of landmass erosion is due to natural causes. Human activities, including construction, farming, mining, and even recreation, are responsible for the other 70 percent.

In parts of Mexico and Central America, the population is growing. Forests have been destroyed. People have allowed their animals to **overgraze**. Both practices have led to severe soil erosion.

In southern Europe, soil erosion has appeared on hillsides because of **deforestation** and overgrazing. Europeans in the north recognized what was happening in the south, so they began a conservation program so the same thing wouldn't happen.

In China, most of the forests have been cut down for wood. Serious erosion developed, and the quality of the water supplies dropped as soil was deposited in rivers and streams. The Huang He, or Yellow River, riverbed rose. Now the river often floods, which causes even more erosion along its banks.

Many people in northern Africa raise herds of sheep and goats. Overgrazing along the southern edge of the Sahara Desert has damaged much of the land. Since the soil and sand's protective vegetation has been removed, erosion is common. Because droughts have kept the arid lands dry, erosion has caused the southern border of the Sahara to increase at a rate of almost 30 miles a year.

Human activity has increased erosion. It will be up to people to think of ways to control this problem.

6

Controlling Erosion

Erosion is natural, and weather plays an important part in the process. Without human activities, losses of soil through erosion and the formation of new soil would balance each other in most areas.

People can't change the weather, but they can control what they do. Rapid population growth and intensive use of land have quickened the natural processes of soil erosion. Soils, which require centuries to form, may be eroded away in a single rainstorm or wind storm because of improper land use.

Conservation

Since the early 1900s, more emphasis has been placed on conservation. Until then land was overused, misused, neglected, and destroyed.

Conservation

Conservation is the management, protection, and wise use of natural resources. Sunlight, water, soil, minerals, plants, and animals are examples of natural resources.

Since the great erosion problems of the 1930s, the U.S. government has taken action that will help farmers prevent a tragedy like the Dust Bowl from occurring again. In 1933, President Franklin Roosevelt formed programs to provide jobs for unemployed people. One of the programs was the Civilian Conservation Corps (CCC). Workers planted trees and built dams to control floods. Both of these activities helped curb erosion.

Also in 1933, the Tennessee Valley Authority (TVA) was created to protect the resources of the Tennessee Valley. The region had suffered from severe soil erosion caused by flooding. The TVA planted trees and built dams.

In 1935, President Roosevelt established the Soil Conservation Service. This agency taught farmers to use better techniques to protect rich farmland soil. Farmers began planting trees and leaving patches of natural vegetation between their fields and on unplowed areas. They used new plowing and planting techniques.

Farming Efforts

Today, farmers still plant trees to provide windbreaks and vegetation to slow the runoff from rainwater. Plants protect the soil from the direct force of raindrops and wind. Their roots form an underground network that holds the soil in place. Plants also absorb some of the rain so that less runs off the land.

President Roosevelt with members of the Civilian Conservation Corps

After harvesting, many farmers leave stalks and other plant matter on top of the soil. This holds the soil in place throughout the winter. The stalks and matter also decay to provide more natural nutrients for the soil.

Instead of leaving fields idle, some farmers plant grass, alfalfa, or other thick crops to protect the soil.

Materials

two trays—tray A should contain only soil. Tray B should have soil with grass.
newspaper
several books
paper cup
small pitcher of water

Procedure

1. Place the trays on a newspaper-covered table. Tilt both trays with several books so that one end is higher than the other. Both trays should be tipped equally.
2. Poke several small holes in the bottom of the paper cup.
3. Hold the cup about 12 inches over the high end of Tray A. Slowly pour the water into the paper cup to create "rain." What happens to the soil? Why?
4. Now hold the paper cup over the high end of Tray B. Slowly pour the water into the paper cup. What happens to the soil? Why?
5. Write your observations and conclusions in your science journal. Relate your findings to what you think occurs when rain falls on soil that contains no plants. Why does this happen? Soil erosion occurs when unprotected soil is washed away by rainfall. Plants prevent soil erosion by stabilizing the soil with their root systems.

Industrial Efforts

Many environmental groups pressure the government to make stronger laws concerning air pollution. Factory owners are working on reducing the amounts of pollutants that they release into the air. These pollutants mix with water vapor to form sulfuric and nitric acids. They then return to Earth as acid rain.

Weather Forecasting

Weather is a very important factor in erosion. It can have a devastating impact. Too much moisture causes flooding. Too little moisture results in droughts and dry land. Hailstorms can wipe out an entire crop and leave fields barren.

Weather is unpredictable. Forecasters are usually accurate when they predict the weather for several days into the future. But what about a month into the future?

Today forecasters study trends and patterns and make use of new technology. Soon they may be able to forecast the weather for not just tomorrow or next week, but possibly for next season or even next year. Then humans might be able to lessen the effects of erosion caused by weather.

Barometer

Conclusion

Earth is in a constant state of change. Erosion moves matter from one place and leaves it in another. It shapes Earth with elements such as water, ice, and wind.

Some ask, "Should all erosion be stopped?" "Are the results of erosion always bad?" The answer is no.

The results of erosion can sometimes be beautiful enough to become national monuments or parks. Yet acid rain, poor farming techniques, and land clearing threaten to wear away Earth's surface, layer by layer, at a faster pace than it can be replaced.

Environmentalists work daily to try to "save the Earth." They encourage people to change how they farm, manufacture, and even live. Scientists and geologists study, monitor, and **regulate** erosion and its causes. They continually update and record their findings. Based on their recommendations, we can prevent the harmful effects and protect nature.

36

Internet Connections for Erosion

teacher.scholastic.com/dirtrep/ erosion/index.htm
Join the Dirtmeister as he explains how the forces of erosion change the world in which we live.

billnye.com
Bill Nye, the Science Guy, explains erosion in episode number 94. From the homepage, click on Episode Guides. Then go to Planetary Science/Earth Science/Erosion.

www.bright.net/~double/erode.htm
See one young boy's weathering and erosion experiment. Then try some others that are also listed.

http://www.brainpop.com/science/ earth/weathering/index.weml
Tim, Toby, Cassie, Rita, and Bob the Ex-Lab Rat explain weathering with experiments and a movie.

www.oznet.ksu.edu/fieldday/kids/ welcome.htm
This site is part of the Kansas State University Research and Extension Service. Water and wind erosion is discussed in relation to farming practices.

64.146.2.54/studentservices/ iecayouthresourcelist.htm
Need a science project for erosion? Check out these links to other sites from the International Erosion Control Association.

www.nrcs.usda.gov/feature/ education/
Meet S. K. Worm. This official worm of the Natural Resources Conservation Service answers questions about soil and soil conservation.

Glossary

absorb (uhb SORB) to soak up a liquid

acid (AS id) relating to a corrosive compound that usually dissolves in water

condense (kuhn DENS) to lose heat and change from a vapor into a liquid (see separate entry for *vapor*)

contract (kuhn TRAKT) to shrink or become smaller

debris (duh BREE) fragments of rock broken down by a powerful natural force

deforestation (dee for es TAY shuhn) act of removing the trees from an area of land

deposit (duh POZ it) to form a layer of sand, sediment, or other substance in one place (see separate entry for *sediment*)

drought (drowt) long period of extremely dry weather when there is not enough rain for crops to grow

embed (im BED) to become deeply lodged in something

environmental (in VEYE ruhn men tuhl) relating to the natural world, especially to its conservation

evaporate (i VAP or ayt) to change a liquid into a vapor, usually by heating (see separate entry for *vapor*)

excess (eks SES) more than is usual

expand (iks PAND) to become larger in size

geologist (jee OL uh jist) person who studies the structure of Earth, in particular rocks, soil, and minerals (see separate entry for *mineral*)

glacier (GLAY sher) large body of slow-moving ice and compacted snow

gully (GUHL ee) channel or small valley carved out by heavy rainfall

mineral (MIN er uhl) inorganic (not living) solid substance that is found naturally in rocks

mouth (mowth) place where a stream or river enters a sea or lake

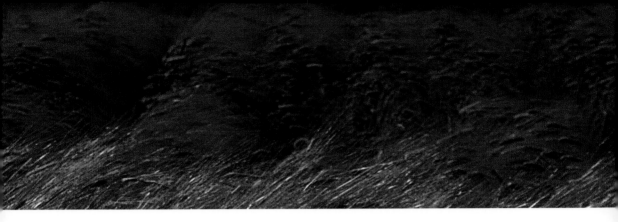

nutrient (noo TREE uhnt) any substance that provides nourishment

overgraze (oh ver GRAYZ) to eat grass and other green plants in a field to the point that vegetation is harmed and can no longer support animal life (see separate entry for *vegetation*)

particle (PAR ti kuhl) very small piece of something

pollute (puh LOOT) to cause harm to an area of the natural environment—air, soil, or water—by introducing harmful substances

regulate (REG you layt) to control something and bring it to a desired level

rivulet (RIV you luht) small stream of flowing water

schist (shist) rock whose minerals are aligned in one direction so it can be split into layers (see separate entry for *mineral*)

sediment (SED i muhnt) material eroded from rocks that is transported by water, ice, or wind and deposited elsewhere (see separate entry for *deposit*)

topsoil (TOP soyl) upper fertile layer of soil from which plant roots take nutrients (see separate entry for *nutrient*)

vapor (VAY per) gaseous state of a liquid

vegetation (vej uh TAY shuhn) plant life

weathering (WETH er ing) breakdown of rocks and minerals by natural processes (see separate entry for *mineral*)

Index